THREE
BY THE SEA

THREE
BY THE SEA

by Edward Marshall
pictures by James Marshall

SCHOLASTIC INC.
New York Toronto London Auckland Sydney

ISBN 0-590-26582-2

Text copyright © 1981 by Edward Marshall.
Illustrations copyright © 1981 by James Marshall.
All rights reserved. Published by Scholastic Inc.,
555 Broadway, New York, NY 10012, by arrangement
with Dial Books for Young Readers, a division of
Penguin Books USA Inc.

12 11 10 9 8 7 6 5 4 3 2 1   6 7 8 9/9 0 1/0

Printed in the U.S.A.   24

First Scholastic printing, March 1996

The art of each picture consists of a black ink line-drawing
with three overlays prepared in ink and pencil and
reproduced in gray, blue, and yellow.

For Paula Danziger

Lolly, Spider, and Sam

had a picnic on the beach.

"I'm as full as a tick,"

said Lolly.

"Me too," said Sam.

"Hot dogs and lemonade

always hit the spot."

"Now for a swim," said Spider.

"Oh, no," said Lolly.

"Not so soon after lunch."

"Rats," said Spider.

"How about a nap?" asked Sam.

"Oh, no," said the others.

"Naps are no fun at all."

"Very true," said Sam.

"Want to hear a story?" asked Lolly.

"I brought along my reader."

"A fine idea," said her friends.

"Then let's begin," said Lolly.

LOLLY'S STORY

The rat saw the cat and the dog.

"I see them," said the rat.

"I see the cat and the dog."

The dog and the cat saw the rat.

"We see the rat," they said.

And that was that.

"Is *that* the story?" said Sam.

"Is that *all*?" said Spider.

"That's it," said Lolly.

"I didn't like it one bit,"
said Sam.

"Dull," said Spider.

15

"I can tell a better story than that!" said Sam.

"I bet you can't!" said Lolly.

"Can!" said Sam.

"Let him try," said Spider.

"Okay," said Lolly. "But it has to be about a rat and a cat."

"Easy," said Sam. "Sit down."

Lolly and Spider sat down. And Sam began his story.

"A rat went for a walk,"
said Sam.

"So what?" said Lolly.

"Let Sam finish his story,"
said Spider.

"Thank you," said Sam.

18

SAM'S STORY

A rat went for a walk.

"What a fine day," he said.
"The sun is shining
and all is well."

Soon he came to a shop.

"My, my," said the rat.

"What a pretty cat.

And I have never had a cat."

"I will buy that cat

and have a friend," he said.

And he went into the shop.

"I want a cat," he said.

"Are you sure you want a *cat*?" asked the owner.

"I am sure," said the rat.

"And I want that one."

"That will be ten cents,"
said the man. "If you are *sure*."

"I am sure," said the rat.
"Here is my last dime.
Give me my cat."

The rat and the cat left
the shop.

"We will be friends," said the rat.

"Do you think so?" said the cat.

"Well, we'll see."

The rat and the cat sat
in the sun.

"What do you do for fun?"
asked the rat.

"I like to catch things,"
said the cat.

"That's nice," said the rat.

"I am hungry," said the cat.

"How about lunch?"

"A fine idea," said the rat.

"What is your favorite dish?"

"I do not want to say,"
said the cat.

"You can tell me," said the rat.
"We are friends."

"Are you *sure* you want to know?"
said the cat.

"I am sure," said the rat.

"Tell me what you like to eat."

"I will tell you," said the cat.
"But let us go where
we can be alone."

"Fine with me," said the rat.

The cat and the rat
went to the beach.

"I know," said the rat. "Fish."
"You like to eat fish."

"Not at all," said the cat.

"It's much better than fish."

"Tell me," said the rat.

"I just *have* to know."

"Come closer," said the cat.

"And I will tell you."

"Yes?" said the rat.

"What I like," said the cat, "is..."

"...CHEESE! I love cheese!"

"So do I," said the rat.

"And I have some here."

"Hooray!" said the cat.

"And now we are friends."

So they sat on the beach

and ate the cheese.

And that was that.

"Very sweet," said Lolly.

Spider looked cross.

"I did not like the end," he said.

"It was dumb."

"Then *you* tell a story,"
said Sam.

"Easy as pie," said Spider.

"And I'll make it *scary* too."

SPIDER'S STORY

One day a monster

came out of the sea.

He had big yellow eyes.

He had sharp green teeth.

He had long black claws.

And he was really mean.

It was time for lunch,

and he was hungry.

On the beach he saw some cheese.

"Blah!" he said. "I hate cheese."

And he went on by.

Soon he came to a rat.

The rat did not hear him.

He was asleep.

"Too small," said the monster.

And he went on by.

Down the beach

he came upon a cat.

But monsters don't eat cats.

So he went on by.

Monsters really like kids.

On toast!

"There must be some tasty kids on this beach," he said.

Very soon he saw some.

"Yum!" he said. "Two boys
and a girl! Nice and juicy!

I'll have *them* for lunch!

But if they see me,

they will run away."

So the monster was very quiet.

He tiptoed up behind the kids.

They did not hear him.

They were telling stories.

He crept closer...

and closer....

"Look out!" cried Spider.

Lolly and Sam jumped ten feet.

"Help!" they cried.

"He's going to eat us!"

But there was no monster.

No monster at all.

Spider laughed himself silly.

"Did you like it?" he asked.

"Oh, yes," said Lolly and Sam.

"But we were not scared a *bit*."

47

"How about a swim?" said Spider.

"That's a fine idea!"

said his friends.

And that was that.